THE DINOSAUR DETECTIVES

IN THE RAINBOW SERPENT

BOOK FOUR

STEPHANIE BAUDET

Published by Sweet Cherry Publishing Limited
Unit 36, Vulcan House
Vulcan Road
Leicester, LE5 3EF
United Kingdom

www.sweetcherrypublishing.com

First published in the UK in 2016
2020 edition

ISBN: 978-1-78226-385-2

© Stephanie Baudet 2016

Illustrations © Allied Artists
Illustrated by Illary Casasanta
Cover design by Andrew Davis

The Dinosaur Detectives: The Rainbow Serpent

The right of Stephanie Baudet to be identified as
the author of this work has been asserted by her in
accordance with the Copyright, Designs and
Patents Act 1988.

Printed and bound in India
I.IPP001

CHAPTER ONE

Matt Sharp held the fossilised egg in his hand. This egg was small, as dinosaur eggs went. It was about the size of a turkey egg, so he could easily hold it in one hand.

He closed his eyes as the familiar shimmering, swimmy feeling began to happen, although after all this time he was not afraid. This was the exciting bit: where he was able to visualise the dinosaur that would have emerged from this egg!

The scene opened up in front of him and, for the first time, he could smell the fresh forest aroma as well as seeing it. This was no tropical scene though. He was not able to feel his surroundings, but he knew that it was cold. There was a cool clarity about the light, and the shadows were long as if the sun was low on the horizon. This

egg had been found in Australia when that country had still been joined to Antarctica, and was much further south than it was now, below the Antarctic Circle.

'Well?'

From a distance he could hear his dad's impatient question, and he concentrated on the creature that was standing in front of him chewing on some foliage, a tendril of which trailed from its mouth.

It stood on its two powerful back legs and had particularly long feet, with three toes pointing forwards and the fourth backwards, like a bird. The front limbs were shorter and the thin fingers ended with sharp-looking curved claws. The tail was long and tapered, and seemed to help the creature balance.

As Matt watched, the dinosaur stopped chewing and seemed to be listening, its large eyes alert. Then, in an instant, it was off, jumping away at tremendous speed, reminding Matt of a kangaroo.

Matt found himself once again in his living room at home. He gently placed the egg on a table.

'What is it?'

Matt almost smiled at his dad's enthusiasm. 'It's about a metre long, has large eyes, and can

7

move very fast. It's a herbivore – and Dad, I can smell things now! Soon I bet I'll be able to reach out and touch the dinosaurs!'

'Before you do that, make sure it's a herbivore – and a small one,' said Dad with a grin. 'It sounds like a fulgurotherium. They were extremely fast – it was their main defence from predators. Did it have large feet? Can you give me more details?'

Matt did so. This helped his dad to get the details correct when he did his paintings. He was not only a palaeontologist, but also a palaeo-artist, and one of world renown. Until now, people thought his beautiful drawings were based solely on fossils, but maybe soon Matt's unique ability to visualise them would become public knowledge. Matt wasn't sure how he felt about that yet.

Now that Matt was twelve – nearly thirteen – he was allowed to accompany his dad on expeditions around the world to excavate dinosaur fossils, particularly eggs, which were his dad's speciality.

'Do you think that's what the opalised fossil is, Dad?'

His dad shrugged. 'Could be. It hasn't been identified yet, but our task is to see if there is an egg nest, too. Imagine opalised eggs!'

'What's an opalised egg?'

It was Jo, Matt's cousin. She came in through

the open door from the patio and flopped down onto the sofa, picking up her phone and flicking through for messages.

Matt frowned. Was she really interested, or was her phone more important? Sometimes it was hard to tell with Jo.

Dad, though, was not going to pass up the opportunity to talk about his favourite subject.

'Australia is the world's foremost source of opal,' he said. 'It's formed from sediments from a huge inland sea millions of years ago. Fossils have been found that have either been covered in opal or where opal has formed in the cavity left by the creature when it decayed. Those are solid opal. So far they've mostly found small creatures, though. Not many dinosaur fossils.'

Jo was staring at Dad, her eyes wide. 'Wow! Solid opal! How beautiful that would be?'

'Do you know what opal looks like?' asked Matt, he doubted she knew what she was talking about.

'Yeah, Mum has an opal ring. Dad bought it for her fortieth birthday last year. It's quite a big opal and all fiery red and green. Well, it's big for jewellery, but an egg ...' she was speechless at the thought of such a thing and Matt couldn't help but smile. He had to agree; it would be awesome.

CHAPTER TWO

The flight had taken just a couple of hours. The long journey from the UK was over, thankfully, and they had spent two nights in the city of Adelaide, on the south coast of Australia. Now they were coming in to land in a flat, treeless landscape that stretched from horizon to horizon. Opal country.

Matt gazed out of the aircraft window at the vast expanse of red earth. Now though, as they approached the town, he could see that the ground was covered with piles of soil.

'Look!' said his dad, and Jo stretched in front of Matt to see what her uncle was pointing to. 'Each one of those mounds of soil indicates someone's mine. They're called mullock heaps.'

Matt knew that, and he looked disdainfully at

his father. Jo might not know it but he did. Surely Dad knew that.

'It's where you go noodling,' said Jo, looking at Matt with a small smile of triumph.

Matt grinned. Just the word amused him. 'Can we noodle while we're here, Dad?'

'Of course! I'm sure we can find time for that. We don't want to miss the opportunity of finding that elusive big opal, do we?'

Wow! How cool was that? Sifting through the mullock heaps with a sieve and finding some 'colour', as the miners and locals called it. The idea of noodling excited him almost as much as searching for the dinosaur fossils. He wasn't going to get 'opal fever' though, if that's what they called it. Matt knew about the gold rush and how people had risked everything in their vain hope of striking gold. It became an obsession where some people lost all sense of reason and rationality.

There was a bump as the aircraft wheels touched the ground, and soon they were taxiing to the small terminal building. The three of them had more luggage than anyone else, having come from the UK, but it didn't take long to unload.

But as they emerged from the building, a group of men stood on the pavement watching them.

Matt felt uncomfortable under their relentless stare. There was no doubt about it; the men were watching them, and they were not happy. He could feel their silent anger aimed at them like an invisible cloud.

It was a relief to get into a taxi and head for their hotel, along a wide, dusty main street with a few shops on either side. The taxi driver seemed friendly enough, and unloaded their cases outside the hotel.

The hotel held another surprise. It was underground!

The front entrance was on the street, but the hotel itself was dug into the hillside.

'It's so cool inside,' observed Jo as they walked into the lobby.

Matt refrained from pointing out that it wasn't that hot outside. It was August, and mid-winter here, although it was certainly not cold: just warm, like an early summer's day back home. It was usually Jo who made remarks about the weather, and he wasn't going to start that too.

As usual, Matt and Dad shared a room, while Jo had a small room to herself. The rooms were comfortable, although obviously they had no windows. There was plenty of ventilation though, by means of metal tubes that pierced the roof.

'I thought this might amuse you,' said Matt's dad as they dumped their cases and went back into the lobby. 'Staying in an underground hotel. There are quite a few underground houses around here, too.'

'And if you want an extra room, you just dig it,' said Matt.

'That's what they're doing in my room,' said Jo, joining them. 'It's not exactly an extra room, but they're digging out an en-suite. I might help if I've got nothing to do.'

'Come on,' said Matt's dad, heading for the door. 'We're meeting the palaeontologist in a café somewhere near here. I'm ready for a drink. What about you two?'

There hadn't been time to mention the men at the airport, but they worried Matt. 'We don't seem very popular here, Dad,' he said, as they made their way through the hotel.

'I noticed that, but maybe it wasn't about us at all.'

But Matt knew that it was.

'One thing's for sure, Uncle Alan,' said Jo as they emerged into the bright sunshine.

'What's that?'

'Frank Hellman couldn't possibly find us here.'

Matt looked at his dad, whose expression told him that he wouldn't bank on it. That rogue seemed to know their every move, though so far

15

he had not got away with stealing any fossils. But would Dad's luck run out …?

With their unpopularity here, they didn't need Frank Hellman as well.

CHAPTER THREE

The palaeontologist was called Bill Stewart. He was tall and thin with fiery red hair and pale skin, and was sitting at a table at the back of the café. As they entered he stood, smiling broadly, and obviously guessing who they were.

'Alan Sharp!' he said, stretching out a hand in greeting. 'I'm Bill Stewart. Great to meet you!'

They shook hands and another man, who had been sitting with him, stepped forward. He was an aboriginal man, dressed in a bright yellow shirt and jeans. He shook hands with Matt's dad too.

'My assistant, Jimmy Burrabindi,' said Bill.

Jimmy flashed them a friendly smile. He nodded at Matt's dad and then looked at Matt and Jo. 'Hey! You brought your kids – that's great!'

Well, that made a change, thought Matt. They were usually frowned upon.

They all sat down and ordered drinks.

'I can't wait to see the opalised fossil,' said Jo, and Matt had to stop himself from scowling at her. He saw his dad frown. This was not the time to make their presence felt, it was Dad's opportunity to speak with his colleagues. He and Jo should be keeping a low profile.

Once again, he resented Jo coming, but it had become the routine now, as her parents, both doctors, couldn't take time off in the school holidays to care for Jo. He had to admit that she was sometimes good company, but at other times she risked them not being allowed to go on the expeditions at all.

Bill Stewart looked at her in a friendly way, holding up his hands. 'I'm afraid I don't have it in my pocket,' he said with a chuckle. 'Opal is very valuable, and a piece that size has to be kept in a bank vault.'

Of course it did!

'We're a little worried about a group of men outside the airport,' said Matt's dad. 'They just stood and glowered at us as we came out.'

Bill nodded, 'I'm not surprised. We're not too welcome around here with some of the miners. Blokes scrape around in the dirt in those dangerous tunnels for months hoping to strike it rich. Then when someone does, strangers from elsewhere come and confiscate it. They don't see the value of ancient fossils.'

Matt's dad glanced at Matt and Jo.

'Oh, they won't hurt the kids,' said Jimmy. 'They're basically decent blokes but when they get struck by the fever they become obsessed.'

'Opal fever?' asked Matt.

'Yeah, that's right,' said Jimmy. 'It's like gambling. You're sure you're going to hit the jackpot tomorrow and if you give up and leave, you might just have been a centimetre away. Look, why don't I show you kids around the town?' Jimmy finished his drink. 'Let these blokes talk business.'

They finished their drinks and followed Jimmy outside.

He showed them some underground houses. 'They're cool in summer and warm in winter,' he said. 'It can get cold at night this time of year. Cold to us anyhow.'

'Have you always lived here, Jimmy?' asked Matt.

'Aw yeah, my people have lived here for thousands of years. No reason to move anywhere else.'

Their tour of the town ended overlooking the mining sites, the once flat earth now covered with mullock heaps, cranes and small digging machinery.

'Can we see a mine, Jimmy?' said Matt.

'Yeah, I reckon,' said Jimmy. 'If you're very careful. They're just holes in the ground. Have you seen the signs? No running. No walking backwards.'

'Why would anyone walk backwards?' asked Jo.

'Yeah well, it's not something I do a lot,' said

Jimmy with a grin. 'But you know when people take photos they step back to get a good shot? Not a good idea here. Look.'

In front of them was a mine shaft. It was about two metres across and had a metal ladder hanging from a thick wooden beam placed across the hole.

Matt carefully looked down but couldn't see the bottom. 'Isn't it dangerous? Do you get cave-ins?'

Jimmy nodded. 'Yeah, it happens.'

'Have you ever found any opal?' Jo looked at him, her eyes gleaming.

'I've done some noodling and got some bits. When we were kids we were always raking through those mullock heaps. Yeah, we get bits

of colour sometimes. I never bothered to stake a claim and dig a hole, though. I prefer to stay above ground.'

Jo looked at Matt. 'I'm not sure I want to join in this fossil hunt if we have to go down there.'

Matt had mixed feelings but didn't feel like sharing them with Jo just yet. He, too, dreaded the thought of climbing down such a narrow hole into the depths of the earth, but he also didn't want to miss out on the excitement.

'I reckon we should get back,' said Jimmy. 'You want to see that fossilised bone of the Kakuru, don't you?'

'Kakuru?' said Matt. 'What's that?'

Jimmy grinned. 'An old Dreamtime story. I'll tell yous about it later, okay?'

Bill Stewart and Dad were in the bank when they met up again. Then they all followed the bank clerk into the vault at the back, through a heavy steel door.

When the fossil was unwrapped, it sat under a brilliant overhead light, gleaming red and green from its magnificent depths. The little group stared silently in awe. Matt could see why people admired it. Then his dad reached forward slowly and picked it up, holding it carefully as if it were made of eggshell.

It was about thirty centimetres long by five wide. In dinosaur fossil terms it was small, but, Matt surmised, very big in opal terms. He would have loved to have touched it but knew better than to ask, and hoped that Jo wouldn't either.

She had apparently realised her previous mistake and said nothing, but couldn't take her eyes off it.

'Who found it?' asked Matt's dad.

'Just a bloke who had come up from Adelaide to do a bit of digging for a week. Beginner's luck,' said Bill. 'Though as I said, he's not too pleased to have had it requisitioned and his mine closed to him. He'll be compensated though.'

'I expect the news of it brought a new wave of fortune-seekers,' Dad said.

'Too right,' said Bill. 'Good for town business though. I'm not from here – I'm from Adelaide, but I've been here from time to time doing a bit of digging. No luck so far.'

'The bug hasn't got you?' said Matt's dad.

Bill shook his head. 'I've got over it. You've got to give yourself a limited time and then walk away. It can rule your life – and even destroy it.'

Matt could see how addictive it could be. Whenever you stopped digging, you would always wonder if you had just missed a strike.

They split up with Bill and Jimmy after agreeing to meet early the next morning to begin the search. Matt was still nervous about going down one of those narrow holes in the ground, but he said nothing to Jo. There was always the thought of Frank Hellman at the back of his mind too. He had been on their trail for the last three expeditions, somehow knowing exactly where they were. Matt suspected that he would be ruthless if he didn't get the dinosaur eggs soon. He had the money to fund his expeditions, Dad had said, and he was hell-bent on getting his own back on someone who was successful, without doing the work himself.

Jo had dropped back to walk with him. 'Do you think your dad is worried?'

'What about?'

'Frank Hellman.'

Matt stopped and looked at her. 'How did you know I was thinking of him?'

Jo shrugged. 'You looked worried, and you've nothing else to worry about, have you? Except the animosity in this town.'

At least she hadn't sensed his reluctance to go down the mine.

'Yeah, well, it is a bit threatening, and as for Frank Hellman, he seems to have spies everywhere.'

'I can't believe he and your dad were friends at university.'

'They weren't friends,' said Matt, 'They just happened to be doing the same course at the same time, just as their fathers had done.'

'We should spot them in a small place like this.'

'That's just it,' said Matt. 'This place has people coming and going all the time. The permanent population is small.'

'Who said? Did I miss something?'

'I did a lot of research,' said Matt, smugly putting an end to the conversation.

CHAPTER FOUR

Matt awoke early the next morning, before anyone else was up. The sunshine beckoned, as well as the new adventure, although it was slightly dulled by the prospect of going down the mine. Matt tried to push the thought out of his mind.

He got up quietly and let himself out.

The town was quiet too, as it was Sunday, and he wondered whether miners took the day off. Probably not.

A slight breeze whipped the red dust up into a twisty whirl that spun off across the plain, and Matt stopped to watch it.

'Never seen a willy-willy before?' a voice said, making him jump.

A boy about his own age stood scuffing at the

ground with one foot. A shock of unruly blond hair framed his tanned face and he squinted at Matt, grinning in a lopsided way.

'What?'

'That spinning dust. You don't know anything, do you? You're with that bloke who's come to look at the dinosaur fossil.'

'Yes,' said Matt. 'He's my dad.'

The boy shaded his eyes as if trying to get a clearer look at Matt. 'Not too popular round here, mate,' he said. 'The best strike anyone's made in ages, and you've come to take it away.'

Matt shrugged. 'Not us. It'll go to a museum here in Australia.'

'Aw yeah, and we'll be going to see it every week. Just hop on a plane ...'

'Are you from here?' asked Matt, ignoring the sarcasm.

'Well, for the moment. My dad came here a year ago and he keeps scratching the earth but she hasn't revealed any colour to us yet, or not much. He keeps hoping, but I reckon he ought to give up. Mum's sick of it here too.'

Matt was drawn to the mine area and the boy

followed. They both stood, peering down into the first mine they came to.

'Better not get too close,' said the boy.

'I can see it's dangerous,' Matt said. 'I'm not stupid.'

'Nah,' said the boy. 'I mean, if the owner sees us he'll think we're ratting.'

Matt looked at him and the boy grinned, raising his eyebrows, 'Robbing from his mine.'

Matt nodded. 'I'd better get back, anyway,' he said, backing away from the hole. Suddenly he remembered what Jimmy had said about walking backwards, so he turned around and cautiously made his way back to the dirt road.

'See ya later,' said the boy. Matt looked back over his shoulder and nodded. The boy sat down at the base of a mullock heap and scrabbled in the soil, letting it run through his hands.

'Will you show us how to noodle?' asked Matt.

'Might,' was the reply.

The mine where the fossil had been found was out at the edge of an area that hadn't been mined yet. A large grey contraption mounted on a truck stood next to the hole.

'It's a blower,' said Bill. 'Although actually it sucks, like a giant vacuum cleaner. People used to lug the spoil up the ladder in a bucket, which was back-breaking work.'

As the group got out of their vehicles and assembled at the rim, Matt saw a man watching them from about fifty metres away. He nudged Jo.

'That's the bloke whose mine it was,' said Jimmy, seeing where they were looking.

Matt felt relief that it wasn't one of Frank Hellman's spies, and he couldn't help feeling a bit sorry for the man who had made such a great discovery, only to have it taken away.

Nevertheless, Matt knew that something was bothering Dad. He was frowning, and he seemed to make a decision.

'I don't want you two down the mine today,' he said. 'Let me get a feel of it first. I know you want to help, but not today.'

Matt pretended to be disappointed and Jo certainly looked genuinely so, but neither of them spoke. Inside, Matt felt himself relax. He'd been in dangerous situations before, but his dread of going down that mine had seemed overwhelming.

Dad glanced at the mine owner, who was still watching them. 'Can you amuse yourselves? Maybe go back to the town and explore. I think there's a good mining museum. Will you be ok?'

Jimmy came to the rescue. 'They'll be right, Alan. This is a safe town, and that bloke and his cronies aren't mad at the kids,' he nodded towards the miner.

Dad smiled and then turned his attention to the mine. After putting on hard hats with lights attached, they stepped onto the ladder one by one and disappeared into the ground.

For a moment Matt stayed to look at the entrance to the mine. He couldn't help imagining all the dangers that lurked below. Matt was afraid for his dad, but eventually he turned and walked away with Jo, back towards the town. There wasn't anything he could do about it now.

They wandered about a bit and did visit the

museum, but Matt struggled to concentrate. His thoughts were with his dad. Although he didn't fancy going down the mine, in some ways he would have preferred to have been there with him.

They bought a drink from the supermarket and swigged it as they strolled back.

'It's like a desert here,' said Jo, kicking at the dry dusty road. 'I'd hate to live here. There's nothing to do and it's miles from anywhere.'

'G'day.' The boy sprang from nowhere. He looked at Jo. 'This your sister?'

'My cousin, Jo,' said Matt. 'What's your name?'

'Brat,' he said. 'Least, that's what Mum calls me. It's Brad really.' He held up a couple of sieves, 'You want to do some noodling?'

Jo was looking sceptically at the stranger, but her face brightened at the mention of the word 'noodling'.

'Cool,' said Matt.

They followed him back to the fossil mine. There was no sign of Dad or the others, but there was some activity in nearby mines.

The mullock heap was huge, and made up of all the earth that had been excavated when the shaft was dug. It towered over them.

'Where's the best place to start?' asked Jo.

Brad shrugged, 'Anywhere.'

'What does opal look like? Can you see the colours?' Jo eagerly took one of the sieves.

'Sometimes. There's potch, too. That's colourless opal and it's not worth much. If people aren't sure, they put it under ultraviolet light. That shows it up.' Brad looked as though he enjoyed showing off his knowledge.

'Oh shame,' said Matt. 'I forgot to bring my ultraviolet light with me.'

They all sat at the bottom of the heap and began putting handfuls of earth into the sieves and shaking them.

The sun became quite hot as the morning drew on and Matt had just put down his sieve and was reaching for his bottle of water, when the quiet was shattered with an enormous explosion. It shook the ground, and a great cloud of dust billowed out of the mine in front of them.

'Dad!' Matt cried.

CHAPTER FIVE

Matt cried out and ran to the mine opening, grabbed the top of the ladder, and began scrambling down. The dust was thick and choking, making him cough and gasp for breath, but he tried to ignore it. His one thought was his dad.

Above, he vaguely heard someone shout, 'No, Matt. Wait! Jo's going for help.'

It was Brad, but Matt ignored him, hardly even registering what he was saying. How could he just sit and do nothing when his dad might be hurt?

As he descended, what light there was quickly faded but still he clambered down, without even knowing how deep this hole in the ground was. He just felt for each rung of the ladder with his foot. The darkness and dust were suffocating, and he could feel his heart thudding as a wave of fear washed over him. It could easily turn into panic if he let it. He must focus on Dad.

What had caused the explosion? He'd heard of gas in coal mines but didn't know about opal mines.

Strangely, he realised now that he could just see the rungs of the ladder in front of him. Then he saw that a glow of light was coming from above. Someone was following him down with a torch.

'Matt!' Brad coughed. 'Matt! Wait!'

He paused until he could see Brad's feet above, and then began to descend again. Matt realised how foolish he'd been: when he reached the bottom of the shaft he wouldn't be able to go anywhere without that light. There was no darkness as absolute as the darkness underground.

'Dad!' he shouted. There was no reply. There was no sound at all except for his and Brad's rasping breath as the heavy dust clogged their throats.

At last, as he reached down with his foot for the next rung, he felt solid ground, and he stepped back from the ladder to let Brad step off, too.

'No good coming down here without a light, mate,' said Brad, shining his torch at Matt. 'You ok?'

'Yeah,' he looked around. There were three

tunnels veering off from the shaft. 'Which way? Do you know?'

Brad shrugged. 'Dunno, but we ought to go down the one with the dust coming out. If they'd been in the other tunnels they would have come back here to escape.'

'What was that explosion?'

'Aw, some stupid bloke in the next mine, I reckon,' said Brad. 'They're supposed to let you know before they detonate, but that home-made explosive is a bit unpredictable.'

Matt frowned, but kept going: he'd ask about that later. He turned towards the tunnel on their right and Brad went ahead with the torch.

The roof was only a few centimetres above their heads and an adult would have to stoop to walk along. The walls were very tight in places, too, making the experience terrifyingly claustrophobic. Several times Matt felt the wave of panic rising in his chest and he had to fight it back. Only his more desperate fear – that his dad was in serious danger – spurred him on.

The dust was beginning to settle, but as they went deeper into the mine, the air became staler.

It wasn't long before they came to the cave-in.

Brad shone his torch over the heap of soil and rock caused by the fallen roof. It stretched from floor to ceiling.

'Dad!' Matt yelled again, tearing at the earth and clawing handfuls away from the sides. He sobbed as he scratched at the enormous heap, knowing he was making little impression on it.

'Matt! Stop! Be quiet and listen,' said Brad, grabbing his arm.

Reluctantly, Matt stopped digging and tried to control his panic and his breathing.

'What's your last name?' asked Brad.

'Sharp.'

'Mr Sharp!' yelled Brad, then gripped Matt's arm to urge him to listen.

Silence.

They both called again, in unison, but there was no reply. Their voices just echoed back at them.

Matt felt sick. Was Dad trapped, or …? He couldn't bring himself to think of the word. If he was trapped, the air supply would run out soon, wouldn't it?

Brad was tugging his arm again. 'We can't do any good here, mate,' he said. 'The rescue blokes will be down with the diggers. It's not the first time there's been a cave-in. It's one of the risks of tunnelling underground. They'll know what to do, and we'll be in the way here.'

The ascent up the ladder was less frenzied than the descent had been, and Matt kept stopping to glance back towards the cave-in. As they emerged from the top they could see a lot of activity around a neighbouring mine shaft. An ambulance stood with its engine idling while a truck with sophisticated lifting gear was slowly backing towards the mine opening. They waited around for a few minutes, Matt hardly able to keep still from worry and fear.

Then, unbelievably, Jimmy's head appeared from the shaft and he clambered out, shaking the dust from himself like a dog.

'Jimmy!' Matt ran towards the man, who turned

around. For the first time since Matt had met him, the big smile had vanished from his face.

'Your dad's okay, Matt. We all are. No thanks to this stupid fella,' he pointed at a sullen-looking man standing between two police officers a few metres away. 'Coulda killed us all,' he put his arm around Matt's shoulders.

A paramedic came up to Jimmy.

'I'm okay,' he said. 'Mr Sharp might need a sticking plaster or two though.'

'Dad!' Matt sprung forward as his dad clambered up the ladder and onto the surface. He looked pale underneath the dust and grime that covered his face. There was a cut on his forehead and the blood had mingled with the dust and formed a brownish rivulet down his right cheek. His eyes had a slightly wild look about them, and darted about until he spotted Matt.

Then he gave a stiff smile.

He said nothing, but reached out and embraced his son.

'Dad! Are you okay? You've cut your head.'

His dad nodded, still not speaking. Someone fetched something for him to sit down on, and a paramedic came forward with his medical bag and squatted in front of him to clean the wound.

When he'd finished, he smiled and nodded. Matt thought that Dad looked a little better, although he was looking worriedly at his arm.

Bill Stewart had also emerged from the mine and came over. He, too, looked shocked and Matt suspected that this was not something he'd experienced before either. Being a palaeontologist was not usually so dangerous, although there were always some risks.

'Are you all right, Alan?'

'Yeah.'

It was more of a sigh than speech, but it was a start, Matt thought.

'Lost my watch,' he added.

Matt breathed a sigh of relief: at least Dad wasn't seriously hurt. Then he became aware of Jo and Brad hovering in the background. 'Thanks for going for help, Jo,' he said, and she smiled.

The three of them were given a lift back to the

hotel, where Matt's dad was advised to rest for the remainder of the day. He lay down on the bed and was soon asleep, snoring softly.

Matt was relieved that his dad was okay, but now that there was nothing more he could do, he felt a bit lost. He'd had a shock too, though it wasn't as bad as his dad's. Quietly he let himself out of the door, went to Jo's room and knocked.

Jo had a small trowel in her hand and was on her knees jabbing at the wall about twenty centimetres up from the floor. A small pile of earth was collecting directly underneath.

She gave a small grin and waved the trowel at the wall. 'The en-suite!' she said, 'and I might find some opal in the process. How's Uncle Alan?'

'Asleep. Do you think you should be doing that?' as soon as that the words escaped his mouth, Matt realised how it sounded: just like a parent! Where was his sense of fun? Where else could you dig out the walls of your hotel room without being in major trouble? He could see that Jo was enjoying herself.

'You'll never get it finished in time,' Matt joked, trying to balance his earlier remark. He watched her for a few moments. 'What will happen when they come to clean the room?'

'I'll just put my suitcase in front of it and drape my clothes over it.'

'Shall we go out?'

Jo turned, 'Where do you want to go? Not much to see in this town.'

He shrugged, 'We can't just hang about digging bedroom walls until dinner time.'

'True.' She put the trowel on the floor and scraped up as much of the soil as she could and put it into a plastic carrier bag. 'I'll dump this outside. Then it won't be so obvious. We've got to find some opal while we're here.' She looked up and her eyes shone. Was this the first sign of opal fever? Matt knew that Jo could get her teeth into issues, but this time he wondered if she might become a victim of one herself.

They wandered around the town. The houses were spaced apart, though nothing much grew in their gardens. Occasionally someone had planted a tree, but otherwise there was very little greenery. Matt thought that here maybe water was too precious to waste on watering plants.

As they were returning past, a pub a man staggered out and spat on the ground in front of them.

'Go home, ratters!' he said, pushing his face so close to Matt's that he could smell his breath.

'Go home or worse things will happen than cave-ins.'

For the first time, it occurred to Matt that the mine explosion might have been deliberate.

CHAPTER SIX

Dad seemed better the next morning, although he was still subdued.

'That roof fall has completely destroyed the area where the fossil was found,' he said gloomily as they sat down to breakfast. 'I wonder whether there is any point in staying here. We'll end up aimlessly digging like everyone else. It'll be a waste of time. And what's more, my watch is lost.'

There wasn't much Matt could say because it was true. He knew that finding any opal was a haphazard process because there were no geological signs, so finding opalised fossils would be even more difficult. And that watch had been an award from the Palaeontology Institute.

Back in the lobby, Dad's mobile rang. While he took the call, Jo wandered over to the reception where the hotel manager was busy on his computer. Matt followed, curious.

'Are there any mines right near the hotel?' she asked.

The manager looked up and shook his head. 'No working mines,' he said. 'This was one of the first areas to be worked, but there aren't any maps. They've all been abandoned now.' He looked towards Matt's dad. 'How is he? I heard about the cave-in.'

'He's okay, thanks,' said Matt. 'It's just that the cave-in covered the area where the fossils were found.

'That's a pity.' The man's smile seemed sincere and he resumed his work, but Matt couldn't help wondering whether he was being sarcastic and wanted them gone, like many others.

'What did you ask that for?' asked Matt, walking away with Jo.

She smiled, 'Come and see.'

Matt could see that his dad was still on the phone so he followed Jo to her room. When they opened the door he couldn't see anything, until she moved her suitcase.

The hollow in the wall was now about forty centimetres across, but instead of more wall behind, there was a gaping hole.

'I've broken through into a mine,' said Jo. 'I thought I'd better check that it doesn't belong to anyone, and we're not likely to meet anyone down there and be accused of ratting.'

'You mean …' Matt stared at her.

Jo smiled and nodded. 'You're not curious?' she said. 'Could you break through into a tunnel and not want to find out where it goes?'

Half a dozen excuses rushed into Matt's brain all at once. No, they weren't excuses, they were good reasons why it would be silly and dangerous to go exploring unused mines on their own. He stared back at Jo. She raised her eyebrows.

'I don't see the point. It's an abandoned mine.'

'But it might lead towards our mine. We've nothing better to do around here for excitement.'

'When?'

'Tonight?'

Matt felt a little surge of excitement mingled with his fear. This wouldn't involve going down a mine shaft, but it still meant crawling about underground.

And if he didn't go, would she think he was a coward? She might tease him about it. He had to summon up his courage and go.

She was still looking at him.

He forced a bright grin, 'Yeah, great!'

Dad appeared at the door. 'That was Bill. They're going to assess the state of the mine and, if it's safe, get a gang of labourers to shift the debris. They're not sure just how much came down.'

When they got to the door to their surprise it was raining hard. Even the hotel manager was standing looking at it. 'It doesn't rain that often this time of year,' he said. 'Or any time, for that matter.'

It was over in a minute, the sun came out, and a vivid rainbow arced across the sky. Bill and Jimmy emerged from the café, looking up.

'It's Kakuru,' said Jimmy, 'I was going to tell yous kids about him.'

'You don't believe in all that rubbish, do you, Jimmy?' Brad had arrived, too, and grinned up at the aboriginal man.

Jimmy grinned back, and Matt thought it would be difficult to annoy him, he was so good-natured.

'Aw not really, Brad, but those legends are in my bones. It's hard to deny them, and I know some of the blokes will be wary of going down that mine, now that he's showed himself.'

They all walked towards the mines as the warm sunshine almost visibly dried up the puddles, but as they passed a café Jimmy said, 'Let those blokes go and look at the mine. I'll buy you kids a drink and tell you about Kakuru.'

Matt watched his dad and Bill go. He wasn't sure whether Dad was ready to go back down the mine. It wasn't Kakuru anyone should be afraid of – it was another cave-in, especially if the rain had soaked down, making the earth even more unstable.

'Kakuru was a great spirit from Dreamtime,' began Jimmy, and Matt ignored Brad rolling his eyes. If he didn't want to hear it, he could leave.

'He was also called the Rainbow Serpent, and he created the rivers and mountains of Australia.

After that, tired with all the effort, he crawled into a waterhole and lay in the cool water. Animals and people alike were careful not to disturb him when they drank at the waterholes, because they didn't want him churning up the earth again. He only came out after a rainstorm when the water was agitated and the sun came out, shining on his beautiful colours as he arched across the sky, to find a home in another billabong.'

'I can see why they named the dinosaur Kakuru,' said Jo, 'when they found the opalised leg bone.'

Jimmy nodded, 'Experts think it might be a new family of dinosaurs, so they had to think of a name for it.'

But hope of finding any eggs was fading, Matt thought. He wouldn't get the chance to actually see a Kakuru in one of his visions. It would be a totally wasted trip.

Brad seemed to read his mind, 'Is your dad going to give up, then?'

'I thought you wanted to see us gone.'

'Not me,' Brad shrugged. 'Makes no difference to me.'

'Matt,' Jo caught his eye, 'I think I'll go back to the hotel after this drink. I want to send some texts to friends.'

'And tell them it's all been a failure?'

She shook her head, 'I've got stuff to do in my room.'

Matt got it then. She wanted to explore the tunnel now.

'Okay.'

'Do you mind if we head back, Jimmy?' Jo smiled.

'Go ahead. I'll join those guys in the mine, see if I can be of any help,' he smiled back at Jo and finished his drink, then they all parted ways.

'See you later then, Brad,' Matt said as they approached the hotel.

Brad shrugged again and sauntered off, kicking at the red dust of the road with his battered trainers. He looked back at them once and frowned.

'I nearly mentioned the tunnel to him,' said Jo. 'He might know where it goes.'

'Why should he? It's his dad who's the miner, Brad only noodles.' Matt looked at her hopefully, 'Why don't we do more noodling? At least we might find a little bit of opal instead of leaving here with nothing.'

'I just thought we might as well explore that mine now instead of tonight.'

Matt followed her reluctantly. There was no getting out of it; he had to face his fears.

CHAPTER SEVEN

'We need helmets with lamps really,' said Jo as they entered the hotel lobby. 'But we don't have any. Torches will have to do. It's an old mine and if the roof hasn't fallen in yet, it's probably not going to.'

Matt had no idea whether that was true or not, and he didn't remind her that there had been a heavy rainfall. He could see that she was bubbling with excitement, and it annoyed him. Once again, he thought about what the trip would have been like if she hadn't come. He could just have spent a pleasant afternoon noodling with Brad. Instead, he went to his room, picked up his torch, and joined her by the opening in her wall. There had been no doubt that torches would be essential on this trip, but they always brought them anyway.

Jo was breaking away part of the wall to make the hole bigger. She didn't seem to have thought about what the hotel manager was going to say. Jo was certainly not helping with the bathroom excavation any more.

With a look around the room, Matt followed her into the tunnel, 'we ought to make marks on the walls so that we don't get lost.'

Jo held up a small screwdriver and Matt wondered where she had got it. That wasn't normally part of the kit. Then again, there were tools lying around all over the place here.

Matt left the decision on which way to turn to Jo, and she turned left, towards the main mine area. The tunnel smelt musty but the floor was fairly clear of rubble and the roof was comfortably high above their heads, so they didn't have to stoop.

As they left Jo's room, the little daylight from the hole in the wall soon faded so that they had to rely on their torches entirely. Jo made marks on the wall with the screwdriver, although there was only the single tunnel so far. The further they went, the more Matt thought that what they were doing was foolhardy. No-one at all knew where they were, although anyone looking for Jo would see the hole in the wall in her room, and that gave him some comfort. He wondered how far they would have to go before either they came to a blockage, or how long it would be before Jo would admit this was a waste of time, and Matt could escape this horrible mine.

As they walked, they swept their torch beams over the walls. After all, they were supposed to be looking for opal, weren't they? But the walls remained dull with the occasional piece of white potch, but no flashes of red or green.

They came to a fork, but again Jo decisively took the right one, and a short time later, a left one.

Jo looked back towards Matt, who tried to remember the turns and felt a flutter of anxiety as they made yet another fork. 'Isn't this exciting?' she said, but even she didn't sound convinced.

This time the tunnel was low and narrow and the air even staler. Matt found that his breathing was heavier, and he could hear Jo up ahead, panting slightly.

'This is really claustrophobic, Jo,' he said at last.

He caught her nod in the beam of his torch, 'Let's go back.'

'Is your curiosity satisfied?'

She nodded again.

The whole thing was a waste of time, Matt thought as they retraced their steps back to Jo's room. As they left the narrow tunnel though, he realised that his heart was no longer thudding against his ribcage. He felt quite calm as he glanced around the main mine area. Maybe he had made a start in conquering his fear of underground tunnels.

'Let's go and see what Dad's decided,' said Matt. This was one expedition that he wasn't enjoying, and he half hoped it would be called off and they'd go home.

At the mine, Brad was sitting at the foot of the mullock heap, noodling. He waved the sieve at them. Not far away, the mine owner stood glowering at them and he shook his fist.

Matt tried to ignore him. Bill had said that he was no danger to them. 'Are Dad, Bill and Jimmy down there?'

Brad nodded, 'But not Jimmy. He got called away to settle some sort of dispute.' He waved a hand back towards the town.

'Shall we do some noodling?' asked Jo.

Up until now Matt would have welcomed her suggestion, but a surge of courage made him shake his head. 'You can. I'm going down to find Dad and Bill and see how bad the cave-in is.'

Jo hesitated, then followed him down the ladder.

The dust had settled now and they soon found the two men.

Matt's dad smiled, 'Bill's had some men working on this and they have almost cleared a way through. One last chance. The rest of this needs to be done carefully so we don't miss anything.'

Matt could see a gap between the tunnel roof and the rubble now, and as they worked it soon grew larger. There were no fossils though, or any other signs of opal that he could see.

But as the group leaned back on their shovels and prepared to go through the hole to the tunnel beyond, Jo gave a cry. Then she reached up and pulled a lump of rock out of the roof.

They all crowded round as she dug away at the loose earth with her fingers and pieces flaked off the smooth surface underneath. A curved surface that gleamed red and green in the light of their headlamps.

'Jo!'

Matt could hear the choked-up sound in his dad's voice. He wasn't usually so emotional, but Matt guessed that the earlier shock was still affecting him.

Then Matt heard something and looked up. Further towards the exit shaft he could make out some moving shadows, 'Dad!'

'Hand it over!' It was the mine owner.

Bill stepped forward. 'Look, mate, we explained. You will be compensated, and named as the finder of the fossils …'

The man laughed. 'I am being compensated. Hand it over.' Two more men stepped out of the darkness, both carrying picks on their shoulders.

Matt's dad was still for a moment, then he came to a decision. He took the egg from Jo's hands and gave it to the miner. 'Where is Frank? Is he here?'

'He gets claustrophobia. He paid us well to do the job though,' the man smirked. Then all three men turned and headed for the shaft.

No-one spoke. Everyone stared at each other as they listened to the men's boots clang up the metal ladder. Then there was another metallic rattling sound and Bill ran forward. The rest of them followed.

Then they all stared up the shaft towards the small circle of daylight above.

Only there was no way of reaching it, because the men had taken away the ladder.

CHAPTER EIGHT

There was silence amongst the group. Matt sneaked a look at his dad and realised that the previous day's experience was still affecting him. He looked pale and drawn.

'We should shout,' said Bill. 'All together. There must be someone nearby who will hear us.'

But their shouting brought no welcome faces to the hole above, which was growing dimmer: either dusk was beginning to fall, or another storm was brewing.

Matt looked at the walls of the shaft. They were smooth, bored out with a special machine rather than dug with shovels or small diggers. There was no way anyone could climb up without mountaineering gear. They didn't even have a rope, and the shaft was about ten metres deep.

Jo looked at him with worried eyes. Matt was glad that she was no wimp. She had proved that on other expeditions, although he still found it hard to accept her presence.

Matt's dad retreated from underneath the shaft and slumped down onto the ground, head in hands. At least he wasn't showing signs of a claustrophobic panic, although Matt noticed that his hands were shaking.

'We could go back beyond the cave-in. There might be a way out that way,' suggested Jo.

Bill looked at her. 'This place is a maze of old tunnels. We don't want anyone getting lost. Best all stick together.'

They sat for a while, until they heard a faint pattering sound, and Matt realised that it was rain coming down the shaft. He held out his hand, looking up, and a fat raindrop hit his cheek.

'We have to do something,' he said, going back to the others. 'Jo's idea was good. We need to see if there's another way out. We won't go far.' He looked at his dad: he had his eyes closed and was not going to forbid him to go. Bill said nothing either, but he looked at them anxiously as Jo got to her feet.

Beyond the cave-in they followed the tunnel some way until it split into two.

'I'll go this way,' said Matt. 'I won't go far, but I'll keep shouting. Then I'll come back and we'll do the same thing the other way.'

Jo nodded.

Matt set off on his own and immediately felt very alone. The tunnel was very small and he wondered how grown men moved through here and tolerated the lack of space. Matt couldn't help thinking about the sheer weight of the earth and rock above him, if the roof of the tunnel were to give way, he would be crushed instantly. As if on cue, a noise to his left made him flash his torch up quickly. A little flurry of stones had slid down from the roof into a heap on the floor. Was the rain causing it to be unstable?

He kept calling and Jo replied, but there came a point when he knew he had to turn back. If the roof caved in here ...

Seeing the glow of Jo's torch gradually get brighter made him relax and smile as he caught up with her. 'Your turn,' he said.

Jo went, leaving him alone again. Her calls

became dimmer and he knew they would have to give up and go back to Dad and Bill. It was too risky to just keep going, deeper and deeper into the mine system.

'Matt!' This was no ordinary call from Jo. He set off, almost at a run, expecting the worst. Matt was breathless when he caught up with her, but Jo was standing smiling and pointing her torch beam to something on the wall of the tunnel.

It was a mark made by a screwdriver.

Bill took a bit of convincing when they tried to explain about the hole in Jo's bedroom wall and their previous exploration, but eventually he and Matt's dad got to their feet. They followed the two back past the cave-in and into the right fork of the tunnel.

They almost missed the hole in Jo's wall because her light was off, and the hotel receptionist looked surprised when they all emerged into the lobby, looking dusty and hot.

Bill began punching Jimmy's number into his phone.

'The egg!' cried Matt. 'But how will they get away?'

'By plane,' Bill said. 'I'll get on to air traffic control and stop them taking off.'

'If they haven't already,' muttered Matt. He took off out of the door with Jo following. He had no idea how he was going to stop a plane, but he had to do something. Frank Hellman was not going to win.

It was still raining lightly and the sky looked thunderous. A figure intercepted them. It was Jimmy.

'Bill called me. Where are yous kids going?'

'We have to try to stop the plane, Jimmy.'

'What are you going to do, stand on the runway?'

At that moment, the sun broke out and instantly a vivid rainbow arced across the sky. Jimmy looked at it in awe. 'Kakuru!' he said, his step slowing as he gazed upward.

Matt had no time for legendary tales now, he kept running. They were nearing the airstrip and he could hear the sound of a small aircraft's engine. Then he saw it.

The plane was taxiing to the end of the airstrip ready for take-off. So much for alerting air traffic control! He doubted that anyone employed by Frank Hellman would let something like that stop them. The pilot would have been well paid and there were no other aircraft around.

The three of them stopped as they reached the edge of the runway. It was too late. There was nothing they could do now.

The plane had turned and its engines were revving ready for take-off.

At that moment, the black cloud overhead burst and a deluge of rain fell. Matt had never seen rain like this. It drenched them in seconds, and almost forced them to the ground with the sheer weight of it. It drenched the runway, too, which quickly became a lake.

The aircraft's engines quietened as the pilot throttled down. They could see the whole plane shaking with the onslaught of water. There was no way it could take off until the downpour stopped and the runway cleared, which probably wouldn't take long in this dry, thirsty land.

But it was long enough for Bill and Matt's dad to hammer on the fuselage. Soon Jimmy, Matt and Jo had joined them, along with a few men who probably just wanted to join in the excitement.

This plane was going nowhere.

Brad was there too, and he looked sheepishly at Matt and Jo.

'I think this is my fault,' he said.

'What do you mean?' Matt frowned.

'This bloke just paid me to watch you and tell him if you found anything.'

Matt started to speak, but couldn't think of the words. Jo looked at Brad, visibly hurt by his actions.

'Why would you do that?' she asked.

'He said he was a reporter and wanted to write your story and you'd be famous. How was I supposed to know he was just some thief?'

Matt nodded.

'So who is he?' Brad asked.

'He's a rival of Dad's. He wants the fame and the money but without doing any of the work. But once again he has lost out. I hope he won't try again. Do you think that explosion was intentional?'

'But why?' said Brad. 'They wanted you to find the fossil, didn't they?' He shook his head. 'I told you, blokes use home-made explosives. It's cheaper.'

Matt frowned at the stupidity of some adults.

Brad reached into his jeans pocket. 'They found this.' It was Dad's watch. 'It's no good to me, anyway.'

Matt frowned at Brad. Was he saying that if it had been any good, he would have kept it? Who could you trust? He took the watch silently. Dad would be pleased anyway.

But Jimmy was beaming. 'What did I tell you fellers?' he said. 'That Kakuru is a strong spirit. He can stop planes.'

Matt smiled up at the aboriginal man. Maybe there was something in his folk tales.

The egg was unbelievably beautiful and Matt had to force himself to close his eyes for the vision.

The shimmering began and the egg became light in his hands as the scene opened up in front of him.

Again, he could tell that it was cold, from when Australia was part of Antarctica. The creature in front of him was standing at the edge of a vast lake or sea, and dipping its beak into the water, drinking. It was about two metres high and looked

more bird-like than any other creature Matt had seen so far. Its long, sinewy legs were built for speed, but Matt noticed the powerful beak. This was almost certainly a carnivore.

The kakuru lifted its head as if sensing his presence, and looked in Matt's direction, but it was obvious that it couldn't see him. It was about to dip its head and drink again when it must have heard something, and Matt did not yet have that ability.

In a split second, it took off at tremendous speed, back into the sparse trees scattered across the vast plain.

For the first time, Jo had been present while Matt had his vision, and she looked as eager as his dad to hear what he had seen.

'It was a kakuru,' he said. 'It's like a giant flightless bird, although it had what looked like primitive feathers on its back.'

Matt was glad to see that the sparkle had returned to his dad's eyes. His hands twitched, not from shock this time but, Matt thought, from an eagerness to pick up a pencil and start drawing.